LEGEND OF THE
DRAGON
SLAYER

WRITTEN BY
BRANDON MULL

ILLUSTRATED BY
BRANDON DORMAN

SHADOW
MOUNTAIN

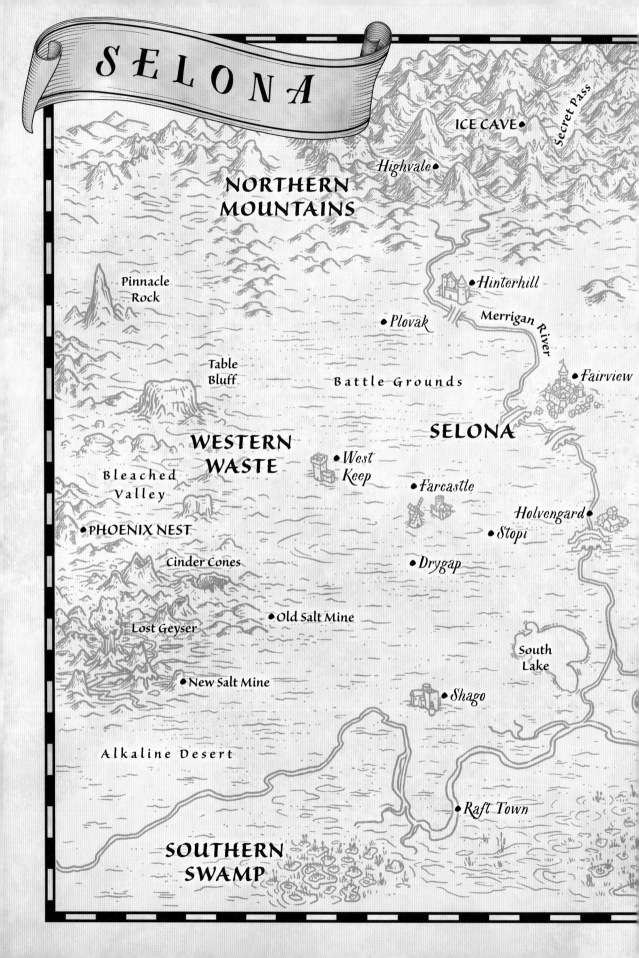

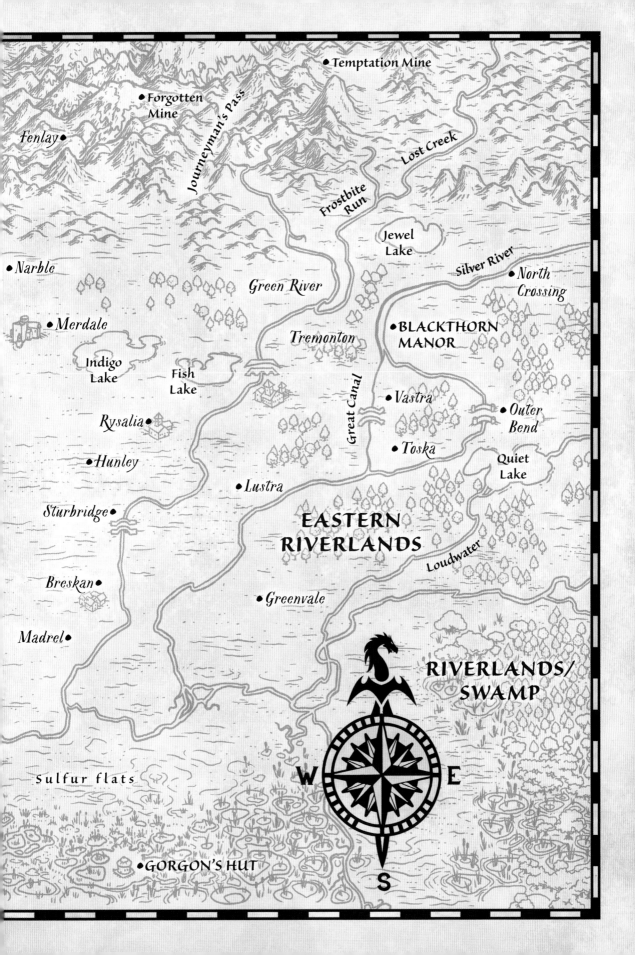

To Chris Schoebinger, who got all of this started.
—BM

To my dad, who can always be found helping those
in need of rescue from life's dragons.
—BD

Book endsheets by JojoTextures/Shutterstock.com

Text © 2021 Brandon Mull
Illustrations © 2021 Brandon Dorman

Visit us at shadowmountain.com

Library of Congress Cataloging-in-Publication Data
(CIP data on file)
ISBN 978-1-62972-849-0
Printed in China
RR Donnelley, Dongguan, China   12/2020
10   9   8   7   6   5   4   3   2   1

LEGEND
OF THE
DRAGON
SLAYER

Long ago, before the world had been properly mapped, King Titus feared for the kingdom he ruled. His beloved realm of Selona enjoyed modest prosperity but was hemmed in on all sides by terrible dangers. To the north, fierce yeti guarded their icy peaks. A merciless vampire haunted the eastern waterways. Access to the southern swamp was impeded by the arcane powers of the gorgon. And in the west, a deadly phoenix scorched his rocky domain.

GORGON

One day in the late spring, the king issued a proclamation: "Selona is growing, but we lack room to expand. My engineers believe we could drain the swamp to the south if only we had safe access. If any man will overthrow the gorgon, I shall grant him the title Earl of Farcastle, along with the associated estate and all pertaining lands, including the mill and the village of Drygap. This offer will stand for the next three days."

Many in the nation of Selona were astonished at the news, for the earldom of Farcastle was among the most prosperous in the kingdom, and though the recently deceased earl had left no direct heirs, the majority assumed the property would pass to one of many surviving nephews. But in Selona, the word of the king was law, and the people waited to see what brave soldier would come forward to claim the prize.

On the first day, many a seasoned soldier was heard grumbling that if he were ten years younger, he would slay the gorgon simply on principle. And plenty of tenderfoot soldiers were heard boasting that after gaining a bit more experience, they would make short work of the threat to the south and then donate the earldom to orphans. But not a single person accepted the challenge.

On day two, the proclamation was repeated by commanders to their companies, who encouraged the best of their men to rise up and accept the challenge of the king. Wives spoke of the opportunity to husbands, fathers

repeated the challenge to sons, and sons fantasized with friends about becoming heroes. When it came to actual volunteers, a drunkard made some vague boasts before staggering away, and a child of seven years tried to sign up until his mother carried him off, but not a single viable applicant came forward.

By day three, the king and his closest advisers began to worry that perhaps the bravest and best of the men of Selona had already attempted to dispose of the threats and failed, leaving behind none bold enough to fill their boots. Near the end of the third day, as the shadows grew long across the town square, an unlikely candidate approached to volunteer.

Konrad, the cobbler's son, was a tall and gangly youth of seventeen. Given to reading more than to action, he had taken up three different apprenticeships only to get dismissed—twice for trying to invent new processes before mastering the basics, and once for talking too much. He was liked well enough by the children who listened to his stories, but many in the older generation felt sorry for the cobbler, whose only offspring seemed a lazy dreamer.

"I may be untested, and I admittedly lack training as a soldier, but I have a willing hand and strength to bear a sword," Konrad said. "I have wrestled with my impulse to step forward since the proclamation was issued, but I can resist no longer. I will slay the gorgon, though I have neither weaponry nor supplies."

After a stunned silence, and some muffled laughs from bystanders, the recruiters realized this might be the only offer they would receive. So, after the sun went down, Konrad was ushered to stand before the king. The candidate was met with graciousness on the surface and despair behind closed doors, for nobody expected the untried youth to succeed where seasoned mercenaries had failed. Nevertheless, Konrad received a horse, leather armor, new boots, a dagger, and a short sword. More imposing armaments were offered, but they seemed cumbersome to Konrad, who also rejected the weight of a helm and a shield.

The following day at first light, Konrad rode away, leaving behind the cheers of the village and the tears of his mother. Not one person expected to see him again, and, besides the cobbler's household, nobody bothered to mourn him. Weeks went by and the days grew hotter, leaving his departure mostly forgotten until, late one blistering afternoon, Konrad returned, gaunt, bedraggled, clothes soiled and torn. Once his identity had been established, the beggarly figure was escorted into the castle to recount his tale before a small, impromptu audience, including the king.

"I left my horse at the brink of the swamp and proceeded on foot, squelching through mud that gripped to the knee, eventually swimming more than walking. Whoever endeavors to drain that swamp has a mighty labor ahead. I will not tell all the tales I could of leeches and snakes, of quicksand and spiders, of pagan totems and scattered bones. Let it suffice to say that after languishing in fetid water for days, my body an exhibition of rashes, bites, and sores, I discovered an expanse of deep water in the midst of the bog.

"Out toward the middle of this pond, I spied a primitive hut adrift on a wooden raft. Human skeletons dangled from crude rafters. I approached with caution, though an unseen splash hinted that my presence was no mystery. My friends will tell you that I am a standout swimmer, but as I stroked toward the hut, strong hands seized me and pulled me deep, to my supposed doom.

"I awoke caged at the rear of a warm room that reeked of unsavory spices. My hair still wet, I'd been stripped to the waist, boots and weapons gone. From the slow rotation of the room, I understood that I was now inside the hut I had identified.

"A foul cauldron frothed in the center of the room, and beside it coiled a grotesque woman. From the waist down she was a huge snake, with a row of sharp quills bristling along the top ridge of her serpent tail. Tightly knit scales sheathed her humanoid torso, and her hideous face was wretched beyond description, with needle teeth and black, soulless eyes. Slime entangled her long, weedy hair.

"Some say the gaze of a gorgon can turn a man to stone. I can only report that, although my body remained fleshy, I lost the ability to move at the sight of her, so great was my loss of courage.

"As I watched the gorgon add bizarre ingredients to her roiling cauldron—crushed herbs and carved stones and pickled organs—her glances at me soon suggested that I would be the final inclusion to her devilish stew. While stirring the hellbroth, she howled out the window, provoking savage replies from the denizens of the swamp. When at last she approached my cage, fiendishly grinning, I withdrew to the rear of the rusty enclosure.

"Why not try to overpower her when she opened the cage door? Allow me to clarify that from her waist to her crown she was taller than I, and I'd sampled her brutal strength in the water. Terror overtook me as her long tail entered the cage, curled about my waist, and withdrew me as if I weighed no more than a bag of straw.

"I have no doubt I would have exited to my death had I not reacted quickly. Driven by instinct more than design, I plucked a quill from the snake tail and plunged

it into the back of her human torso, whereupon she let out a shriek to send nightmares scurrying. Immediately the gorgon dropped me and scrambled from the hut, her lashing tail overturning furnishings and sending crockery crashing. From the doorway, I watched her traverse the pond to a muddy patch of shore, where she turned entirely to stone.

"I will not elaborate on my careful verification that she had indeed become a statue, my treacherous journey out of the swamp, or the successful recovery of my horse. Let me assure you that if you send an expedition deep into the swamp, you will find the pond, the hut, and the corpse of the gorgon exactly as described. In my hand is the very quill I used to stab the villain. I invite the king to handle it if he wishes. The swamp is now safe to be drained, though I warn all who venture therein to beware of natural dangers such as snakes and disease."

In the following days the story was confirmed, and work began to drain the swamp and farm the lands near the brink. Konrad received his earldom amid considerable pageantry, no prouder mother than his could be found in all the land, and the kingdom of Selona rejoiced at their chance to enlarge their southern boundaries.

YETI

few years passed, and the kingdom of Selona prospered. But there were limits to how much swampland could be made habitable, and in time King Titus turned his gaze northward.

A proclamation again went forth: "To the north lie vales to inhabit, slopes where flocks could graze, and mountains to mine. If any man will lead an expedition north and destroy the yetis who patrol the mountain passes, I will name him the Duke of Hinterhill and bequeath to him all lands and titles associated with that fair castle. This offer will stand for the next three days."

The proclamation generated much talk and little action, until near the end of the third day, when Konrad, the Earl of Farcastle, came forward. Dressed respectably, and having filled out admirably since he was seventeen, the young nobleman was taken more seriously than when he had volunteered to go south.

This time, Konrad needed no assistance to outfit

himself, for he had managed his estate well and was able to gather warm clothes and climbing gear, though none in his employ had enough courage to undertake the dangerous mission alongside him. Again, he was alone, and many supposed that he rode to his demise.

Some hunters worried Konrad should have waited for full summer instead of making the trek in the spring. Among townsfolk, reminders were issued that a person could get lucky once, but expecting similar luck again was an affront to fate. But six weeks later, to the astonishment of most, Konrad returned looking leaner, limping slightly, lips chapped, but otherwise unhurt. He was promptly ushered into the throne room, where a large group gathered to hear him.

"I wish I had better heeded some of the elder members of the community, for winter lingers long in the mountain passes. I left my noble mount in a frosty meadow to proceed up an icy slope on foot. There is no need to bore you with complaints of freezing temperatures, blinding blizzards, and rumbling avalanches. I will not dwell upon details of hollowing out snowbanks with frozen fingers to create shelter, nor recount the mournful howls of wolves in the night, nor belabor the perils of scaling crystalline faces of ice.

"After I spent a fierce night huddled in a shallow ice cave, the air became still and the sun peeked out, turning the mountain snowfields into blazing diamonds. That morning, I found a footprint large enough for me

to sit inside. As I encountered more oversized tracks, I began to question whether I wanted to locate a creature who made such large, deep impressions in the snow. Before I could fully refine my intent, the creature found me.

"And it was not alone.

"The yetis had shaggy, apelike bodies and heads like arctic wolves with shortened muzzles. They moved over the snow with ease and showed signs of cunning if not great intelligence. I would have preferred to lead an army of men to attack a single yeti—instead, a pack of them had found me. The grizzliest of bears would seem a modest pet beside the smallest of their number.

"With no hope of prevailing in combat, I attempted to

flee. One glance at their fluid strides told me I would not outrun them, so with a prayer that recklessness might triumph where ability was lacking, I flung myself down the steepest nearby slope. The world spun and powdery snow sprayed haphazardly until I came to rest near the mouth of a cave. The mountain vibrated with the roars of the yetis as they bounded down the slope after me.

"Lacking superior options, I dashed into the opening and soon discovered the cavity to be no minor snow tunnel, but rather a long and winding cave that burrowed deep into the rock of the mountainside. Although the darkness deepened as the entrance receded, still I opted to plunge ahead blindly in hopes my pursuers would not follow. Though generally the cave was roomy, my heart swelled with gratitude when I passed through any narrow opening that might hamper their pursuit.

"Once the darkness became complete, my progress slowed dramatically, not only because of unseen obstacles on the cavern floor, but because it soon became impossible to anticipate where I would find the next opening through which to advance. Before long, I could not tell which direction I was facing. The subterranean atmosphere, though not warm, was well above freezing, and when my heavy coat became a burden, I shrugged it off.

"The bellows of the yetis echoed through the cave, reflecting horrifically off unseen stone surfaces. Fumbling through my belongings, I found flint and steel, and then

a small oil lamp. Frantic sparks led to modest illumination, and I rushed deeper into the cavern.

"By the mellow light of my lamp, the yetis behind me were not yet visible, though their caterwauling seemed to come from all directions. I knew the light made me an easy target, but I needed the glow to advance and realized that the yetis might track me as easily by smell as by sight.

"I believe that at first, the yetis did hesitate to follow me underground. As I progressed, the roars from behind drew rapidly nearer. I began to run recklessly, fearful of turning an ankle, but more frightened of being torn limb from limb.

"Beyond a narrow passage, I reached a vast chamber decorated with stalactites and stalagmites and littered with stones. Not halfway across the broad floor, I saw several yetis appear behind me, lamplight glinting off ferocious teeth and eyes. Their triumphant bellows assaulted my ears, and I noticed creaking and cracking from above. A hasty glance showed webs of fissures in the uneven ceiling where chandeliers of stone dangled precariously.

"My last hope was to find an aperture in the wall large enough to accommodate me but cramped enough to prevent the yeti pack from following. I remember a surge of regret that I would not cheat death as I had in the swamp but would instead perish alone in a dark cavern within a remote mountain.

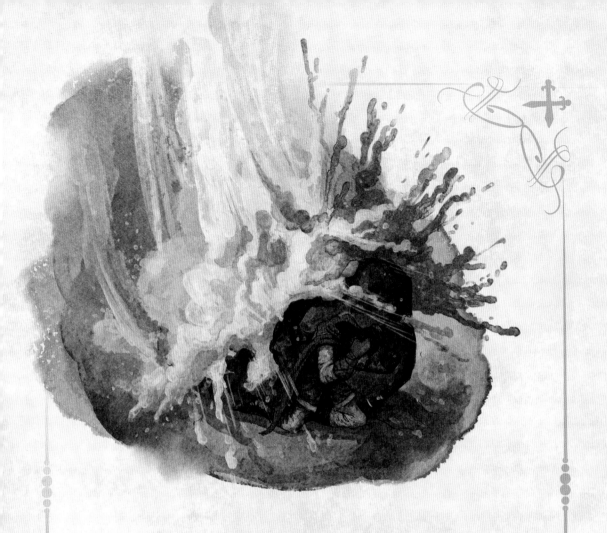

"And then the roof collapsed with a thunder that overpowered the yowls of the yetis. I dove for cover in the lee of a large boulder, which almost certainly saved my life, for though most of the collapse occurred behind me, a multitude of stone fragments scattered wildly around the room. Dust saturated the air as a pair of aftershocks followed the main cave-in. I kept my face to the ground, hands over my mouth and nose to filter my breathing, and still I seemed to inhale mostly particles.

"To my dismay, after the pounding ceased and the rocks settled, the roaring of the yetis persisted. I doubted I had much time before they found their way to me through the rubble and the polluted air. I considered extinguishing my lamp, which for the moment revealed only a brown curtain of dust. As seconds passed, and the roaring came no nearer, I noticed it displayed an uncommon uniformity.

"Hesitantly, I began to relax, and then to hope. After the worst of the dust cleared, I emerged from my shelter beside the boulder. Clambering over the detritus on the cave floor, I found my way to a view of a stunning, underground waterfall—the source of the endless roar.

"Returning to where the ceiling of the cave had fallen, I searched for evidence of yetis in the massive jumble of stone. At one edge, I found a head and an arm protruding from beneath a misshapen boulder. None of the other yetis were visible, and no others appeared to threaten me.

"Evidently, the whole pack lay entombed beneath the rockfall. I had unwittingly led them into a perfect trap, where their savage bellows disturbed an equilibrium made fragile over time. My instinct to flee and survive had accomplished what I could never have hoped to achieve with my sword.

"I had brought my quill from the swamp with me for luck, and it reminded me to claim another prize. As you can see, I used my dagger to remove a fang from the partially exposed yeti and brought it back as evidence. I conducted more explorations of the mountain passes after the events inside the cave, and though I nearly met my end from cold and avalanches, I saw no further indications of yetis. You are welcome to conduct your own investigations, but today I pronounce the northern mountains safe to inhabit."

By the time summer was hot and the snows had released their grip on all but the loftiest peaks, the cave was found, along with the rockfall and the partial skeleton of a yeti. Some of the more adventurous from Selona moved to the mountains as herdsmen or to support logging and mining operations. Using funds from his earldom and newly acquired duchy, Konrad invested in many of these ventures, and though some failed, others paid off handsomely, making him second only to the king in wealth.

VAMPIRE

More years passed, and though the northern mountains granted many resources, they offered limited space for new settlements, and the winters were fierce at high altitudes. Before long, the eyes of King Titus strayed eastward.

A proclamation went forth: "The eastern river lands have ample fields and forests to inhabit and waterways to harness for power and irrigation. If any man will go and vanquish the dread vampire, he will have my blessing to pursue the hand of my daughter, Princess Lilianna. The offer becomes void at the end of three days."

The debate in town primarily concerned whether Konrad would come forward or be content having thwarted death twice and gained so much. Some could not imagine a man of his position risking everything for any reason. Others could not envision a man of his character resisting the urge to again prove his valor. All agreed that a chance to win the hand of Princess Lilianna would be enough to tempt any man, especially since she already seemed to favor Konrad.

The Duke of Hinterhill kept his own counsel and let the town wonder until he came forward on the third day, wholly equipped and in the full bloom of manhood. Court gossips spoke of the approving glances Konrad received from the princess before he departed. Several young men boasted that they had been on the verge of accepting the challenge but that Konrad had narrowly beaten them to the opportunity. But, as on previous adventures, no man offered to accompany him.

When Konrad rode away to best the dread vampire, the majority who worked with him or for him voiced their expectations that he would return. Others reminded the public that luck had played a role in his former victories, and they recounted gruesome tales of the vampire and his sinister exploits in the eastern reaches. Wagers were placed about whether Konrad would again survive, with the majority lamenting that the duke had finally taken one risk too many. But those who bet on his success were rewarded in hardly more than a fortnight, when Konrad rode back into town looking not only unharmed but unruffled. This time the king summoned his court to the town square to hear the tale before a huge crowd.

"I see no need to regale you with the hardships met along the way to Blackthorn Manor. I won't remind you how overgrown the former paths through the forests have become, or the variety of wild beasts roaming that friendless territory—not merely boars, wildcats, and bears, but enchanted creatures as well, clever satyrs and devious nymphs, not to mention the river trolls.

"At length I established camp in the abandoned village of Tremonton, where owls and badgers have replaced men and women. I was struck that the town must have emptied suddenly, for I found tables set for meals, half-completed handicrafts, and plows deserted in the fields. Of people I saw none, save a single jabbering madman who escaped into the woods at my approach.

"Those who know the legends may be interested

to learn that I found Blackthorn Manor exactly as described, upon a slender island in the midst of the Silver River. The stone bridge from the riverbank to the manor was in good repair, and the gates into the fortified residence stood open. The entire scene appeared much too inviting for my liking, but for the thickets of pikes topped with human skulls.

"I approached the manor under the noonday sun, carrying a wooden spear and several wooden stakes. For luck, I also had the gorgon's quill and the yeti's fang. Beyond the gate, I found the courtyard tidy, though the walls were overgrown with ivy. The elegant stronghold appeared utterly derelict. I noted no bones, nor blood, nor signs of violence, though I did not forget that outside were skulls enough to fill an ossuary.

"Spear held ready, I entered the manor. Progressing from room to room, I flung open curtains to admit daylight. Except for a film of dust interrupted by occasional mouse prints, all appeared in order. I detected no evidence of looters—the rooms appeared fully furnished and decorated, without so much as a broken window. This was troubling, because the gates stood open and no door within the manor was locked. Some unseen threat must have held potential interlopers at a distance.

"Toward the end of my disquieting tour of the manor, I located a stone stairway descending into an ancient cellar. Before reaching the bottom step, by the light of my torch I beheld the beginnings of not a cellar but a

crypt. A dragging scrape of stone against stone from the darkness beyond my light brought me to a halt. I was already retreating up the stairs when I heard the crash of a heavy slab, presumably the lid of a sarcophagus.

"I bolted for the courtyard and did not look back until I stood in the full light of day, wooden spear held ready. The fiend came to the doorway, grotesquely human with hairless, pallid skin and jutting bones. Though he wore no shirt, his tattered pants looked to be made of fine fabric. Fierce eyes glared out of a gaunt, knobby head. Tendons stood out on the back of long hands as contorted fingers twisted and jerked.

"Keeping out of the direct sunlight, the abomination studied me, then beckoned with a gesture. I unwittingly took several steps toward him before resisting with a major effort of will. As I backed away, I saw hate and desperation flash into those baleful eyes, and I realized the creature was starving.

"The vampire beckoned again, but with less effect. Baring sharp teeth, the unholy atrocity charged into the sun after me. Fumes rose from his bubbling flesh as the sun seared it, and his violent shriek set my teeth on edge as the fiend approached with alarming speed.

"I raced out through the gates and onto the bridge with the vampire closing fast. Turning at the last moment, I planted my feet and leveled my spear. My assailant flailed forward, blinded, snarling, sizzling, and I impaled his upper chest beside his shoulder only to have the spear wrenched from my grasp.

"The vampire pawed at the spear, screaming, and while his back was turned to me, I plunged a stake just to one side of his spine. I cannot confirm how much of the damage was caused by my attacks, and how much depletion resulted from exposure to direct sunlight and his malnourished state, but the wretched creature dissolved into a cloud of foul particles.

"I stood for a time in disbelief that I had survived. Catching my breath and gathering courage, I returned to the crypt and investigated the vaults and sarcophagi within. None of the desiccated bodies I uncovered

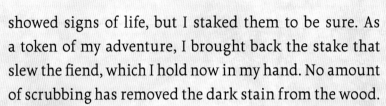

showed signs of life, but I staked them to be sure. As a token of my adventure, I brought back the stake that slew the fiend, which I hold now in my hand. No amount of scrubbing has removed the dark stain from the wood.

"I am relieved to announce that the vampire of Blackthorn Manor is no more. The eastern reaches are reopened to development."

Once again, the story was verified, and the kingdom of Selona gained new industry and territory. Villages were rebuilt, roads refurbished, mills constructed, bridges raised, farms irrigated, and trees felled. Expansion was somewhat limited by impenetrable forests and wildlands, and certain groves were avoided where satyrs frolicked and nymphs dwelt, but overall the kingdom of Selona enjoyed a new era of greater prosperity. Some unknown wit labeled Konrad the Legender, since he had ended three long-standing legends, and the name spread.

The Legender courted Princess Lilianna, and, in time, their affection deepened into a true and abiding love. The kingdom rejoiced when they were married amidst much fanfare. Lilianna birthed two daughters, who received the doting attention of their father until the fateful day when the king approached Konrad in private.

PHOENIX

The final threat to our kingdom is the phoenix of the western waste," the king explained. "The waste holds salt mines, as you know, along with our best trade routes. If we can be rid of the phoenix, the kingdom will be secure, and my reign a success. Age has made me weary, and I am desirous enough to be rid of this final scourge that, if you will destroy the phoenix, I will step down and deliver my crown to you."

"I will accomplish your wish," the Legender replied, "not only in order to secure the throne but out of respect for your desires as my king and my father."

A proclamation went out that the Legender would venture forth on one final mission, and at last the people of Selona believed he would succeed. Konrad had been lionized into a folk hero capable of anything, so destroying the phoenix seemed like a feat he might undertake simply for recreation. Few were shocked at the offer of the king to step down, since Konrad had wed his eldest daughter. Some cautious voices warned that a phoenix was no creature to trifle with, but when Konrad rode away to the west, his departure was met primarily with merriment and high expectations.

As weeks passed, the people of Selona began to doubt. After the first month, Princess Lilianna could often be found weeping in her garden. But after nearly three months away, the Legender returned, hair and

beard grown out, skinny and sunburned, but very much alive. He spoke his last tale from the castle balcony to a sea of onlookers that spread beyond the sound of his voice.

"Some of you may recall I ventured west into arid wasteland with my trusty steed and a pack mule in tow. As I beheld the stark scarcity of that stony wilderness, I began to carefully ration my stores of food and water. I shall not rhapsodize about scorching sands and sun-baked rocks, or scraggly plants surviving through some miracle of adaptation, or the meager comforts found on the shady side of a bluff. I will skip recounting the abundance of scorpions and venomous vipers or the false promises offered by shimmering mirages and parched gulches.

"I reached a particularly tortured landscape where pools of hot sludge simmered, lava oozed from cinder cones, and towering geysers of scalding steam surged rebelliously skyward. My first glimpses of the phoenix resembled a distant spark in the sky. At night the bird became more distinct, a fiery comet among the stars.

"I tracked the phoenix for days, paying closest attention to where it landed and from whence it rose. I took care not to get too close, but I soon came to appreciate that the fiery bird was at least the size of my horse. I also noted that when hunting or agitated, the phoenix burned brighter, occasionally shedding showers of sparks or exhaling fire.

"My patient observations were rewarded when I located the nest—composed of blackened stones, and large enough to accommodate many full-grown phoenixes. There were no visible eggs, but the phoenix returned to the nest every night. On one occasion I observed a mountain lion stray into the nest, and the phoenix erupted into a blazing inferno. Though the cougar fought fiercely, claws and teeth flashing, the doomed feline was charred beyond recognition and consumed.

"I realized that if I was to have a chance against such a fiery opponent, more patience would be required. It took merely two weeks to find the nest, but I waited nearly two months for a respectable rainstorm, conserving my stores and foraging to survive. Rain is not frequent in that arid landscape, but eventually the air grew humid, leaden clouds filled the sky, and water began to fall.

"I approached the nest warily but with purpose. I did not know when I might get another opportunity to attack in wet conditions. I reached the nest as the downpour intensified, my clothing already soaked. The phoenix glowed faintly, having sought the limited shelter of an overhang, low flames flickering among iridescent plumage. Water pooled at the bottom of the depression.

"I climbed into the nest and attacked the bird with a spear. The phoenix had its head tucked under a wing and did not sense me coming. I drove the spear in deep, then backed away and began firing arrows.

"With a wailing screech, the phoenix blazed brighter,

gouts of flame issuing from where the spear had penetrated and where the arrows struck. The bird came out from its shelter, and the pouring rain hissed as the droplets were vaporized. Falling back, I continued to launch arrows as the downpour quenched the flames. The phoenix collapsed in the pool, wings flapping feebly, and, with sword drawn, I advanced and severed the head.

"The bird took on a peculiar glow, as if an

inferno raged internally, and then collapsed into flaky ashes. As the pile of ash began to absorb water and turn to sludge, I remembered tales of phoenixes being reborn from their cinders. I gathered an armful of sodden ashes, then hurried to the edge of the nest and scattered them. I repeated the process many times, hurling goopy handfuls in various directions.

"I wanted to disperse the remains as completely as I could. I packed some of the soggy ashes back to my horse and my donkey, mixed the remnants with their oats, and fed the combination to them. My horse refused to consume much, but the donkey ate with gusto, perhaps because I had not been generous with the feed until that point. In the spirit of camaraderie, and quietly hoping to perhaps derive some benefit, I also ingested some of the ashes.

"My donkey became sluggish and died the next day. I feared my horse and I might suffer the same fate, but though I endured a debilitating stomachache, we survived. Evidently I scattered the ashes sufficiently, because though the pool at the bottom of the nest turned into boiling sludge, the phoenix was not reborn. I waited several days to be sure. Under the overhang in the nest, I recovered a single magnificent feather, which I display to you now. I declare the threat of the phoenix over and the western waste open to all who care to venture there."

Konrad came down from the balcony, and the crowd pressed forward to view the phoenix feather, easily the

most impressive of the Legender's mementos, glinting red and orange with an inner light. True to his word, within a year the king abdicated, replaced by King Konrad, Lord Protector of Selona. In the following years, Lilianna bore him two sons. His daughters grew tall and fair, and the Legender governed well. Selona prospered under his leadership, free from the major threats that had once frightened the populace and frustrated expansion.

DRAGON

ome might argue that the kingdom prospered too much, for just after Konrad's eldest daughter, Nadia, celebrated her seventeenth birthday, the Rambling Horde approached Selona. Led by the warlord Kula Bakar, known more commonly as the Dragon, the Rambling Horde had been sacking cities for more than twenty years. Before each conquest, the Dragon gave the targeted kingdom a chance to send a champion to face him in single combat. Thus far, no individual had triumphed against him, and no armies or city walls had withstood his horde.

More powerful countries than Selona had fallen to the Rambling Horde, so news of the oncoming riders terrified many in the kingdom. But for every person who quailed, another reminded listeners that Selona enjoyed protection no other country possessed. Selona had the Legender.

When an invitation to combat arrived at the royal palace, King Konrad took the message to his quarters and did not emerge. That evening, Queen Lilianna knocked on his door, and he admitted her. She had never seen her husband looking so disheveled and distraught.

His wife approached and laid a comforting hand on his arm. "Konrad, surely the warlord of the Rambling Horde is no more deadly than the phoenix, no more fearsome than the vampire, no more ferocious than the yeti, and no more dangerous than the gorgon."

"I expect you are right," Konrad said.

"Then you will vanquish him in combat?"

King Konrad dragged both hands through his hair, still thick, but graying. "It is my fondest wish, Lili."

"You are still young and strong," Lilianna said. "You slew four legends. Why not a fifth?"

"I ended four legends," Konrad said, face contorting as if with pain. "But none know the whole tale."

"Tell me," she said.

"The stories about me have grown since I first told them. And they were exaggerations from the start, colored by a young man's fantasies."

"What do you mean?"

"I ventured into the swamp to slay the gorgon, it is true. I took the risk; I braved the leeches and the snakes, the quicksand and the spiders. I found the floating hut, empty, abandoned, adrift. Nearby I discovered the stone gorgon and a single quill. The rest of my tale was invention."

"You never fought the gorgon?" Lilianna exclaimed.

"I never saw her alive," Konrad said. "For all I know, it is possible she never lived. I searched the area until I felt sure there was no threat. I worried that without a fight and a victory, I would not receive my prize, so I embellished."

"But you bested the other three foes," Lilianna said.

"I searched those mountains for weeks," Konrad said. "In the end, I found a cave—that much was true. The cave held a tremendous waterfall, large enough to sound like the roars of a yeti. I overcame freezing temperatures and snowy conditions. I approached that roaring, uncertain of what I would find. I came upon a rockfall and a skeleton of what might have been a yeti, from which I claimed a fang. I debunked another legend and I told another story."

Lilianna regarded her husband, perplexed. "The vampire?"

"I saw satyrs and nymphs," King Konrad said. "I beheld a river troll from a distance. I found the town of Tremonton and Blackthorn Manor, much as I described. The crypt as well. But instead of a vampire, I discovered a sarcophagus full of dust, with the blood-stained stake inside. Who killed the vampire and when, I have no idea. Assuming he ever existed at all."

"And the phoenix?" Lilianna whispered.

"I found what might once have been a nest of rocks, with boiling sludge inside. My horse sampled the sludge, and the donkey tried even more, which prompted me to have a taste. The donkey died and I grew ill. The feather was uncovered beneath a rock as part of my careful search. I had courage, my love, and I was a thorough investigator, but I know little of combat. I ended four legends without fighting or killing anything."

"I must confess, I have long wondered at the grandness of your adventures," Lilianna said. "It comes as little surprise that there was some enhancement to the tales. They have grown on their own since you originally told them."

"I don't believe I ever repeated any of them," Konrad said. "Others have aggrandized them for me, with even more flair than I initially employed."

"You were so young," Lilianna said. "Even with the phoenix."

"I became an earl, a duke," Konrad said. "I married you, gained a crown . . ."

"And you did end those legends. You returned having succeeded. The gorgon, the yetis, the vampire, and the phoenix were all no more. Because of you."

"Perhaps your father would still have made me an earl had I conveyed the precise truth," Konrad said. "And maybe not. Perchance others would have been emboldened as they heard one or two of the legendary enemies were less impressive than expected. We can never know. That history is written."

"But now . . ." Lilianna said.

"Currently I face an actual threat of flesh and bones,"

Konrad said. "A renowned warrior who has never lost a fight. I myself have never drawn blood and know little about the ways of warfare. If I accept this challenge, my incompetence will be exposed and the kingdom pillaged. If I refuse this duel, none will go where the Legender feared to tread. Truly, I wish I had never been born."

"Do not speak such nonsense."

Konrad hung his head. "I feel as if I have already failed."

Lilianna shook her head. "The kingdom prospered because of your courage. You are a good king, beloved by your family and your people. You have governed well. Tall tales about your exploits were inevitable. You just gave them a head start."

"And now I face the consequences of exaggeration. Any choice I make will lead to ruin."

Lilianna folded her arms. "What chance did you have against the gorgon? If she had been real?"

"Little to none," King Konrad confessed.

"What chance against the yetis? The vampire? The phoenix?"

"Very little."

"And yet you ventured out to confront them," Lilianna said. "Alone. Did you know any of them had been destroyed?"

"I expected to encounter them."

"It was not your fault they had already fallen. You have a new foe. Why not ride out to meet him with the same bravery?"

"When I rode south, north, east, and west, I risked only my own life. I was naive enough to have confidence that I would find a way to triumph. But now I am being asked to risk the fate of all Selona on my untested abilities. My people have unrealistic faith in me."

Lilianna hugged her husband. "This is no different from your previous escapades. The only differences are the audience and your fears regarding the consequences.

You still have a willing hand and strength to bear a sword."

"I do believe I would have found a way," Konrad said.

"Don't let your courage fail when it is most needed. Go forward now, in the same spirit as you went forth to rescue the kingdom and win renown, remembering that when a hero is needed, any chance is better than none."

King Konrad gave a nod, resolution in his gaze. "I will prepare."

A response traveled to the Dragon, and the next day the Legender emerged from his castle and rode to the chosen battlefield with a small entourage. Those who watched the procession noted the king's lack of heavy arms and armor. Instead he wore traveling clothes and carried a short sword. The phoenix feather gleamed in his hat, the yeti fang hung from his neck on a cord, the vampire stake and the gorgon's quill were holstered on his belt.

Some whispered he had gone mad, approaching such an important duel so underequipped. Others accused him of overconfidence. A few who were close to him suspected he was playing to his strengths—since Konrad had little formal training in armed combat, and little experience with heavy arms and armor, they reasoned he was staying with what he knew.

Some citizens expressed outrage. After all, the Legender was the last line of defense against a merciless horde. What right had he to enter the fight with no armor? If he wanted mobility, he could at least have worn leather armor, carried a light shield. And why not bring a sword substantial enough to cause real harm?

At the appointed hour, the Legender found the Dragon awaiting him on the field of battle, standing alone, his horde watching from a distance. Kula Bakar was an enormous man, both tall and broad. He wore a great helmet with a cage hiding his face, and he was armored to withstand a landslide. After beholding the size of his sword, it became easy to believe the stories of him chopping a horse in half with a single stroke.

Leaving his attendants behind, King Konrad rode out to meet his opponent. Those near him maintain that Konrad managed to approach with a smile.

"What stratagem is this?" the Dragon called to the Legender. "Do you expect me to strip off my armor and fight you with lesser weapons? This is single combat for the right to sack your kingdom, and I will fight as I have always fought—fully prepared."

"I have everything I need to defeat you," the Legender replied, dismounting from his horse.

"If you lack proper armaments, I will outfit you myself," the Dragon offered.

"I had plenty of weapons and armor at my disposal," the Legender said. "I have brought all I require."

"Is this an insult?" the Dragon asked. "Perhaps you hope to protect your legacy by claiming the contest was unfair? Excuses will not spare your kingdom."

"The insult is your invasion," the Legender said. "I am here to stop you, unless you wish to withdraw."

"Very well," the Dragon said. "Meet your fate as you see fit."

Short sword in hand, King Konrad approached Kula Bakar. The Legender was considered taller than average, but his face was level with the Dragon's mighty chest. Kula Bakar was massive across all dimensions—tall, broad, and thick. The Legender looked like a child confronting an ogre.

"Announce the start of combat at your leisure," the Dragon announced.

"Begin," the Legender said without pause.

Raising his shield and hefting his sword, the Dragon began to circle his quarry. Some who knew his fighting style commented later that it was an uncharacteristically wary approach, perhaps an adjustment to the mystifying preparations of his opponent in anticipation of some trick or trap.

The mobility of the Legender proved valuable as he dodged several attacks. The first time their swords clashed, the Legender lost hold of his blade. The Dragon paused to let him retrieve it, then knocked it from his grasp two more times. After the third drop, the Dragon rushed his opponent. The Legender ducked and whirled, feinted and leapt, avoiding many swipes and thrusts, some by a close margin, until he stumbled and the Dragon planted his sword in his chest.

Pinned to the ground, the Legender twitched a few times, legs spasming, then grew still. Panting, the Dragon withdrew his sword and raised it high. He ended all his fights by decapitation, and this one would be no exception.

But the Dragon staggered back when the Legender was spontaneously engulfed in flame. Confused by-standers raised their hands to shield their eyes from the startling blaze. Out of the intense conflagration emerged King Konrad, his shirt bloody but unburned, his body whole.

"What sorcery is this?" the Dragon asked.

The fire behind the Legender vanished as quickly as it had appeared. With an inhuman roar, the Legender took the gorgon's quill from his belt and stuck it through a gap in the armor near the Dragon's waist.

After the prick, Kula Bakar went rigid, making no motion to dodge or protect himself as the Legender pulled out the yeti's fang and used it to punch a hole in the Dragon's breastplate. Then Konrad plunged the vampire's stake through the hole, deep into the Dragon's chest. The Legender stepped back, and the Dragon remained on his feet for a prolonged moment.

The armor of the Dragon made his fall clangorous on the silent battlefield. Ignoring the enemy horde, the Legender withdrew the quill and the stake, returned them to his belt, and then claimed the Dragon's sword before walking away.

In the years that followed, the Legender offered no explanation of how he had survived, though many inquired. Some guessed he had visited a witch or a wizard who had enchanted the items from his previous adventures. Others proposed that the act of sacrificing his life to save his kingdom activated the powers of his talismans.

All that can be confirmed is that the Dragon fell that day, and the Legender walked away. Witnesses swear that the Legender received a fatal blow and inexplicably burst into flames before achieving victory. Tales spread that he had risen from death like a phoenix and bellowed like a yeti. Stories spoke of Kula Bakar paralyzed by a gorgon's quill and then slain like a vampire, wood improbably penetrating metal.

As always with the Legender, the tales grew over time. Storytellers claimed the leader of the Rambling Horde really was the avatar of a powerful dragon, and they attributed his previous successes to supernatural abilities. Bards sang of a king in Selona who could not die, and of a bloodline armed with mighty talismans.

The Legender gained a new title in the aftermath of his successful defense of Selona—Dragon Slayer. After the Rambling Horde withdrew from Selona, no mortal country attacked the kingdom again. Konrad kept the sword of the Dragon and passed his other talismans to his two daughters and two sons, who also gained renown as Dragon Slayers. The Legender and his four children were summoned to help as dragons became more aggressive in subsequent years.

Over time, the kingdom of Selona gained prominence in the magical community, and the generations who came after Konrad became known as the Fair Folk. Though the Legender did not remain their king, neither was his death recorded. Ever since, as you well know, when dragons have united to plague the world, five legendary Dragon Slayers have stood against them.

Enumeration of Notable Dragon Slayers

LEGENDARY DRAGON SLAYERS

KONRAD, THE LEGENDER
wielder of Wyrmslayer
slew 11 dragons, including one dragon king
A lowly villager who rose to become king
through his heroic adventures.

THE LEGENDER'S FOUR OFFSPRING:

NADIA
—wielder of the gorgon's quill, slew 9 dragons
Nadia never wanted the notoriety that came with a famous family, and, though firstborn, she was the last to become a dragon slayer.

MAGDALENA
—wielder of the yeti's fang, slew 33 dragons
A great lover of the outdoors, Magdalena spent her youth tagging along with her father whenever possible.

MEREK
—wielder of the vampire's stake, slew 49 dragons
A natural leader, most assumed Merek would inherit his father's throne, though that day never came.

GERWIN
—wielder of the phoenix feather, slew 27 dragons
From his youth, Gerwin evoked laughter and smiles wherever he went, except from those who earned his enmity.

OTHER NOTABLE DRAGON SLAYERS

MORISANT THE MAGNIFICENT
—trained by Konrad, wielded Vasilis, slew 17 dragons

Once the chief architect for Zzyzx, Morisant was one of the most powerful and influential wizards of any age. After prolonging his life by joining the undead, he fell out of favor with Dragonwatch.

CLOVER THE UNEXPECTED
—no formal training, slew 19 dragons

The youngest Dragon Slayer on record, Clover used a cattle prod to impale a warty red scrub dragon whom she caught trying to kidnap her sleeping baby brother. She went on to slay dragons employing a surprising variety of weapons and techniques.

BANDERBRUX THE BOLD
—trained by Merek, wielded Imneris, slew 14 dragons

The sole survivor of a goblin massacre in his youth, Banderbrux developed an insatiable thirst to master the art of war. After claiming Imneris by besting Verinon the Devourer, he captained the dwarfen legion throughout the dragon war.

DAKARI THE HARBINGER
—trained by Morisant, wielded the Reapers, slew 15 dragons

Descended from a long line of healers, Dakari made a break with his family when he decided to specialize in combat magic. Shunned by his tribe, he found a new home within Dragonwatch.

BRONWYN OF THE NORTH
—trained by Nadia, wielded Omagion, slew 12 dragons

After hunting polar bears in her youth, Bronwyn graduated to bigger game when she delivered her village from the tyranny of the dragon Kizello.

PATTON BURGESS
—trained by Kumiko, slew 5 dragons

An adventurer of great renown, Patton was a key member of the Knights of the Dawn and a friend of Dragonwatch. He grew up at Fablehaven, where he became the caretaker and married a naiad.

SANCTUARY DRAGON SLAYERS

THE TITAN GAROCLES
—protector of Titan Valley, slew 21 dragons

Garocles has never gone hunting for dragons, but none who have attacked him ever survived. No Dragon Slayer is more feared or less predictable.

THE SOMBER KNIGHT
—protector of Wyrmroost, slew 67 dragons

Of mysterious origin, this undead knight came on the scene during the dragon war and has been dispatching dragons ever since.

SHAYLA THE GIANT
—protector of Soaring Cliffs, slew 13 dragons

The foremost designer of dragon traps, Shayla tends to capture and kill dragons through her ingenuity. She has sold some of her patented equipment to the Giant Queen at Titan Valley.

THE TRICLOPS MOMBATU
—protector of Crescent Lagoon, slew 29 dragons

This overwhelming predator forms when three Himalayan cyclopses combine their power. Mombatu tends to fight first and ask questions later.

THUNDERHOOF THE CENTAUR
—protector of Frosted Peaks, slew 15 dragons

Thunderhoof began by fighting giants, until his life was saved by the giant Thronis. They formed a partnership and began hunting dragons.

KUMIKO
—protector of Isla del Dragón, slew 31 dragons

Raised by the human avatar of the renowned dragon Maru, Kumiko lived for years as a dragon sister. Having come to admire Maru's compassion for all creatures, Kumiko started on the path to becoming a Dragon Slayer when Maru was slain by the rival dragon Jiparo.

THE WINTER SPECTER
—protector of Polar Plains, slew 17 dragons

An expert in weather magic, the sorceress Ariana specializes in manipulating water. With enough ice at her disposal, she fights like a force of nature.

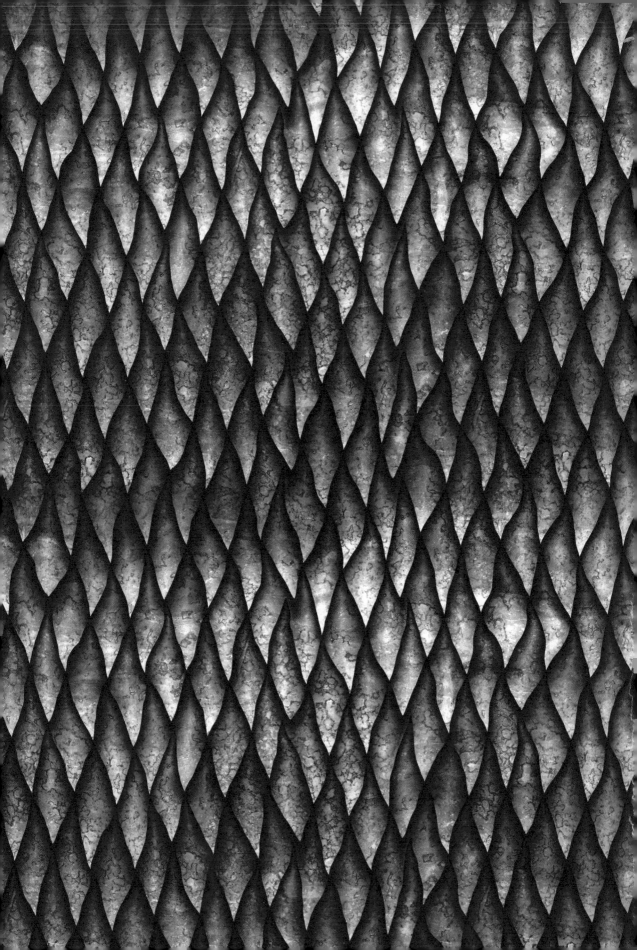